NEWTON
← AND → CURIE
THE SCIENCE SQUIRRELS

DANIEL KIRK

Abrams Books for Young Readers · New York

For Rhoda-Jane and Annabelle

Art for this book was drawn with an ebony pencil on Strathmore drawing paper, then scanned into Photoshop to add color.

Cataloging-in-Publication Data has been applied for and
may be obtained from the Library of Congress.

ISBN 978-1-4197-3748-0

Text and illustrations copyright © 2020 Daniel Kirk
Edited by Howard W. Reeves
Book design by Steph Stilwell and Heather Kelly

Printed and bound in China
10 9 8 7 6 5 4 3 2 1

Abrams Books for Young Readers are available at special discounts when purchased in quantity for
premiums and promotions as well as fundraising or educational use. Special editions can also be created
to specification. For details, contact specialsales@abramsbooks.com or the address below.

Abrams® is a registered trademark of Harry N. Abrams, Inc.

ABRAMS The Art of Books
195 Broadway, New York, NY 10007
abramsbooks.com

BONK!

Newton was sitting under a tree when an apple bounced off his head.

"Why did that apple fall down and not up?" he asked himself. From that moment on, the little squirrel began to wonder how the world worked.

"I wonder why that swing works the way it does,"
Newton said to his little sister, Curie, as they watched
children on the school playground.

"I don't know," said Curie. "Let's go find some nuts to
eat. I'm hungry!"

"Oh, all right," Newton said, but he couldn't stop
thinking about the swing.

Later that day, Newton jumped up on the swing,
the way he'd seen the children do. He sat for a while,
wriggling and rocking. But the swing didn't move.

"What are you doing?" asked Curie.

"Don't you wonder why a swing goes back and forth?" Newton asked. "Why does it go so high sometimes? And why does it work so easily for the children, when it doesn't work for me?"

"Oh, let's not think about that now," Curie said. "Let's play tag!"

The next day Newton passed
by a classroom window.

"Today we'll learn about simple
machines," the teacher said.
"We'll study gravity and force.
And we'll learn about experiments."

As Newton listened, he had an idea.
He decided to try an experiment of his own!

Newton looked around his neighborhood until he found
what he needed to create his own swing.

"What are you doing now?" asked Curie.

"I'm testing an idea," Newton said. "That's called an *experiment*! Pumping my legs gives me the force to move forward. And see how gravity brings me back down again?"

"I want to try," Curie said, and she did.

"What's this?" asked a pair of robins,
who were building a nest in the tree.

"It's science," said Newton.

Curie laughed. "And it's fun!"

The next day, Newton watched some children rocking up
and down on the seesaw. He longed to try it for himself.
At dusk, he went and sat down on one edge of the board.

"What are you doing now?" asked Curie.

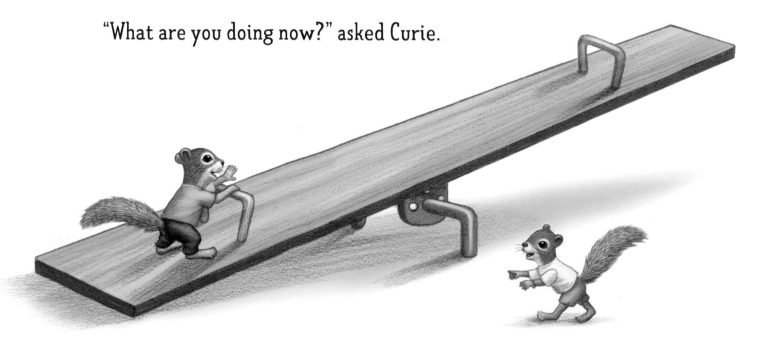

"Come and sit on the other side," Newton said.
"We'll do an experiment!"

Curie sat down, but the board didn't budge.

She jumped up and down, but there wasn't
enough force to make the seesaw move.

"The board is too heavy, and we don't weigh enough," said Newton.

"Humans weigh more than squirrels, so they have more mass."
Curie frowned. "Maybe science isn't for squirrels!"

In the morning, Newton
hurried to the branch above
the classroom window.

He studied the whiteboard and
listened to the teacher explain
another simple machine.

Newton could see that a lever and a fulcrum
looked a lot like a seesaw! That gave him an idea.

Newton searched his neighborhood until he found
what he needed for a squirrel-sized seesaw.

"I'll bet you're making something," said Curie.

Newton smiled. "It's another experiment! The board is a lever,
which increases the force we need to go up and down."

"The rock is for balance. It's called a fulcrum. If we put the rock at the center of the board, we can balance our weights on either end."

"Gravity pulls us down, and we use the force of our legs to push off again."

"Wheeeeee!" said Curie. "And it's fun!"

"That *does* look like fun," said one of the robins.

"It is," cried Newton. "How is your nest?"

"It's all finished," said the bird, "and we have
four beautiful eggs! You should come take a look."

Newton and Curie went to visit the birds in the tree.

"You're so lucky you can fly," Curie said. "Gravity doesn't mean anything to you!"

"Gravity affects everyone," Newton said.

The next morning Newton and Curie went to listen at the classroom window.

"With a wheel and a rope," the teacher said, "you can make a pulley. A pulley makes it easier to lift heavy things."

Curie said, "If we had something big we had to move, that simple machine would be great. But I can carry everything I need in my own paws!"

That afternoon Newton and Curie came to watch the children play. But it was a windy day, so the children stayed indoors.

Just as the squirrels turned to go,
they heard a terrible cracking
sound. A big branch snapped
and toppled to the ground.

"Help!" cried the robins.
"Our nest has fallen!"

"Our eggs are all right," the birds cried, "but we've got to get them back into the tree, where they'll be safe!"

"I've got an idea," Newton said. "Just wait here."

Newton and Curie raced to the classroom window,
which was open just a crack. The children were off
at lunch . . . but they could come back any moment.

"We could use those spools and some string to make a pulley,"
Newton said. "But how are we going to get in there?"

"I've got an idea," said Curie.

"Let's find a stick to use as a lever and
pry the window open so we can get inside!"

The squirrels found a piece of branch and slid one end into the opening.

Then they jumped and jumped on the lever until the window opened . . .

. . . just enough for them to scramble inside and get the supplies they needed.

Back in the tree, Newton fit the spool over a small but sturdy branch. Curie bundled the birds' nest into a cloth and tied it to a long piece of strong string.

"We're making a pulley," Newton said to the birds as
he pulled the end of the string up the trunk.
"We'll use it to get your nest back into the tree."

"Please be careful!" cried the birds.

Once he'd wrapped the string around the spool,
Newton grasped the free end of the string and
jumped from the branch.

Gravity pulled him down, but it wasn't good enough.
The nest was too heavy!

"I know what to do," Curie said, and she jumped onto Newton's back.

Together, the two squirrels weighed enough to pull the string to the ground and lift the bird nest into the tree.

The robins nudged their nest into a safe place.

"Our experiment was a success!" cried Curie.

"The pulley worked!" Newton shouted.

"Soon your eggs will be ready to hatch," Curie said,
"and your babies will learn to fly."

"I wonder how flying defies gravity?" Curie wondered.

"Time for a new experiment," Newton said. "Science is *fun*!"

AUTHOR'S NOTE

I named the squirrel in my story Newton after **Sir Isaac Newton** (1643–1727), a physicist and mathematician who developed the principles of modern physics, including the laws of motion. He is one of the most important and influential scientists of all time. As a schoolboy, I heard the tale that Newton made his discoveries about gravity after an apple hit him on the head. Today we know the apple story is an exaggeration, but that doesn't change our views of Sir Isaac's discoveries. Newton the

Sir Isaac Newton

squirrel's sister, Curie, is named after another famous scientist, **Marie Curie** (1867–1934), who won the prestigious Nobel Prize—twice! She was a physicist and chemist who conducted pioneering research on radioactivity, among many other things.

Marie Curie

Through my Library Mouse books, I encourage children to explore writing for themselves. I want them to become excited about making their own books, telling their own stories. With *Newton and Curie*, I hope young readers will develop a deeper interest in the world around them and in the **scientific principles and laws** that shape our environment. When we learn to think like scientists, asking *how* and *why* things work the way they do, we gain knowledge and mastery that make our lives richer and more rewarding!

WHAT TO DISCOVER IN THIS BOOK

In this story, Newton the squirrel learns how to study the world, which is one meaning of the word **science**. He learns some of the basic laws of *physics*. **Physics** is the science of how things work! When we look at or observe the world, and when we do **experiments** to test an idea, we are practicing science. Newton and his sister, Curie, are behaving like **scientists** when they study the world around them and try to discover why playground equipment works the way it does.

The basic subjects of physics are **matter** and **energy**. Matter is any object that has **mass**, and we measure mass in weight. Newton does not weigh very much; a squirrel normally weighs around a pound. An average seven-year-old child weighs around fifty pounds!

When Newton and Curie listen at the classroom window, they hear many words that come from the world of science and physics. Over time, they learn what these words mean. By learning how and why things work the way they do through observation and experiments, you, too, can get an idea of what it is to be a scientist.

GLOSSARY

ENERGY is what is needed for any activity. There are many kinds of energy, but it is basically the ability of someone or something to do *work*. And by work, we mean what we do to move or change something. When we pump our legs on a swing, we're increasing our energy to go higher.

FORCE is what happens when two objects interact with each other, pushing or pulling. A force can make something speed up, slow down, stay where it is, or even change its shape. A squirrel uses force to carry a nut up into a tree, break the shell, and bite off pieces. We use force to put on our shoes, brush our teeth, and get to school. We also use force to ride a bike, run to the corner, and raise our hands to answer a question in class.

GRAVITY is at work when two objects are drawn toward each other. Anything that has mass has a gravitational pull, and the more mass, the more gravity. That is why the Earth (which is so much heavier than we are) pulls everything down toward it . . . and why the apple that hit Newton on the head fell down from the tree, not up.

A **LEVER** is a kind of simple *machine*, which is an invention or tool that makes work easier. A lever is a bar, balanced on something (called a *fulcrum*) that provides support. Forcing the lever down on one end creates a force pushing up on the other end.

Newton builds his own seesaw with a lever and fulcrum. There are many scientific principles at work in a seesaw. We use our legs to push off, which is a force, and gravity brings us back down again. The length of the lever on each side changes the way work is done. If we weigh more than the person on the other side of a seesaw, staying the same distance from the fulcrum allows us to keep the other person stuck up in the air! But if the heavier person simply moves closer to the fulcrum, it helps balance the weight.

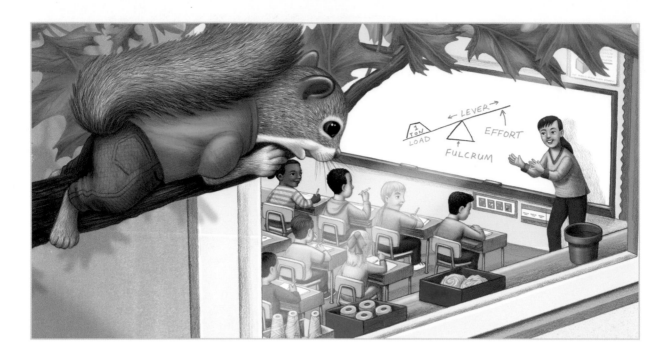

LEARN MORE!

If you are interested in learning more about science, physics, observation, and experiments, there are many websites that explain these concepts in language kids can understand. Below are a few. And if you want to know more, ask your librarian *or a scientist* for help!

Buggy and Buddy: Playground Science for Kids

buggyandbuddy.com/playground-science-kids-exploring-ramps-friction-slide

Easy Science for Kids

easyscienceforkids.com

Kids and Tech

kidsandtech.org

Ology: A Science Website for Kids, American Museum of Natural History

amnh.org/explore/ology

Physics on the Playground

scholastic.com/teachers/articles/teaching-content/physics-playground

Science Development for Kids

pbs.org/parents/education/science/activities/first-second-grade/playground

Science Kids

sciencekids.co.nz